STARTING
PAINTING

Susan Mayes

Designed by Lindy Dark

Illustrated by Terry Burton

Photographs by Howard Allman

Art consultant: Gill Figg

Series editor: Cheryl Evans

With thanks to Shelley Gibbins

Contents

Things you need

This book shows you how to use paint in lots of ways. There are plenty of ideas for things to paint and make using the new skills you learn. On these pages you can see the things you need. You can buy them from an arts and crafts or art supply store.

Paints

There are different kinds of paints. The best ones to use for the projects in this book are ready-mixed paint, powder paint or acrylic paint.

Ready-mixed paint

Powder paint

Water color paints, oil paints and blocks of paint are not good for the projects in this book.

Acrylic paint

Colors

You need a red, a blue, a yellow, white and black. You may have different reds, blues and yellows to choose from. Pick a red called crimson if you have a choice.

If you like, buy an extra red, blue or yellow.

Thickener

You can make paint thicker by mixing in a thickener such as white glue. Add a little to powder paints or liquid paints. (See page 12.)

Glue looks white until you mix it in.

Don't get any on your clothes as it is difficult to get out.

What to paint on

You may like to buy new paper to use. It comes in different sizes. You need letter or ledger size for most of the things in this book.

You could buy bigger pieces and cut them to the size you need.

Ledger size is 11 x 14 inches

Letter size is 8½ x 11 inches

You can use white or colored paper.

Sketchbook

A sketchbook has blank pages that you can paint, draw or stick on. It is useful for testing colors and trying out ideas.

Find out how to make your own sketchbook on pages 24 and 25.

Extra things

You need these extra things every time you paint.

Short plastic pots or a plastic palette, to put paint in

A short jar and a flat plate

Newspaper

Paper towel or a rag

An old shirt or an apron

Brushes

Brushes come in different sizes. Some have soft bristles and some have stiff bristles. It is best to have three soft brushes, for different kinds of painting.

Medium-thickness

Thin, for delicate work

A medium-thickness stiff brush is useful, too.

Thick, for painting big areas

Before you start

Clear a big space and spread out lots of newspaper.

Collect the things in the list at the beginning of the project and the things shown above.

Put your painting shirt on and fill the jar with clean water.

Make a folder

You could make a folder to put your paintings in. Stick two big sheets of cardboard together with sticky tape. Use sheets that are bigger than ledger size.

You could decorate the folder.

Experimenting

You can paint with brushes, but you can use other things too. Collect at least ten different tools that you could paint marks with. Here are some ideas.

Preparing paint

Different kinds of paint need to be prepared in different ways to make them a good thickness for painting with.

Ready-mixed paint comes ready to use. So does acrylic paint in tubs or bottles.

Powder paint is dry until you add water to it.

Acrylic paint in tubes is fairly thick.

Don't fill the pot.

To use ready-mixed paint or acrylic paint in tubs or bottles, just put the color you need in its own pot.

Always put the paint in before the water.

Use a dry spoon

To use powder paint, spoon some into a pot. Drip a few drops of clean water on from a brush. Mix it all in.

Always use clean water for mixing.

To use acrylic paint in tubes, squeeze some into a pot. Mix in drops of water to make the paint creamy.

A lid stops the paint from drying out quickly.

If you have some paint left over when you finish painting, put the pots in a plastic tub with a lid on.

Making marks

Things you need:
Three colors of paint
A big sheet of paper
A collection of tools
for making marks
A plate

Prepare a color. Put some on the plate with a brush, then dip a tool in.

See how many ways you can use the tool to paint marks on the paper.

Brush paint onto big tools.

Change the color you use each time you choose a new tool.

Use different parts of each tool.

You could write the name of the thing you used beside each mark.

Which tools make the biggest number of different marks?

Cleaning tips

Always change the water in the jar if it gets dirty while you are painting.

Clean each tool when you have finished making marks with it.

Wash everything up at the end, to get the paint off.

5

Making new colors

Red, yellow and blue are called primary colors. You can mix them in different ways to make new colors.

1

Draw a fat fish shape on the paper and cut it out. Make the fish about 20cm (8in) long.

2

Press hard.

Draw a pattern on the fish with a yellow wax crayon. The pattern needs about 14 shapes in it.

3

Always wash out the brush and dry it on a rag.

Prepare red and yellow paint in pots. Use a brush to put some yellow on a plate. Paint one shape on the fish.

4

Paint a shape next to the first one.

Add a little red to the yellow on the plate. Mix the colors together. Paint a shape with the new color.

5

Put extra paint on the plate if you run out.

Add a little more red to the color you mixed to change it again. Paint a new shape. Keep making new colors.

Powder paint

If the powder won't disappear, add a tiny drop of water.

Dry powder paint in pots

Dip a damp brush in the yellow powder. Mix it around on the plate. Wash and dry the brush. Then mix in some red.

If you can't make any more colors and your fish has empty spaces, try mixing colors to match ones you have made already.

Can you make a different color for each shape?

A color made by mixing two primary colors is called a secondary color.

More colors

Use a blue crayon to draw a pattern on another fish. Mix yellow and blue to make lots of new colors.

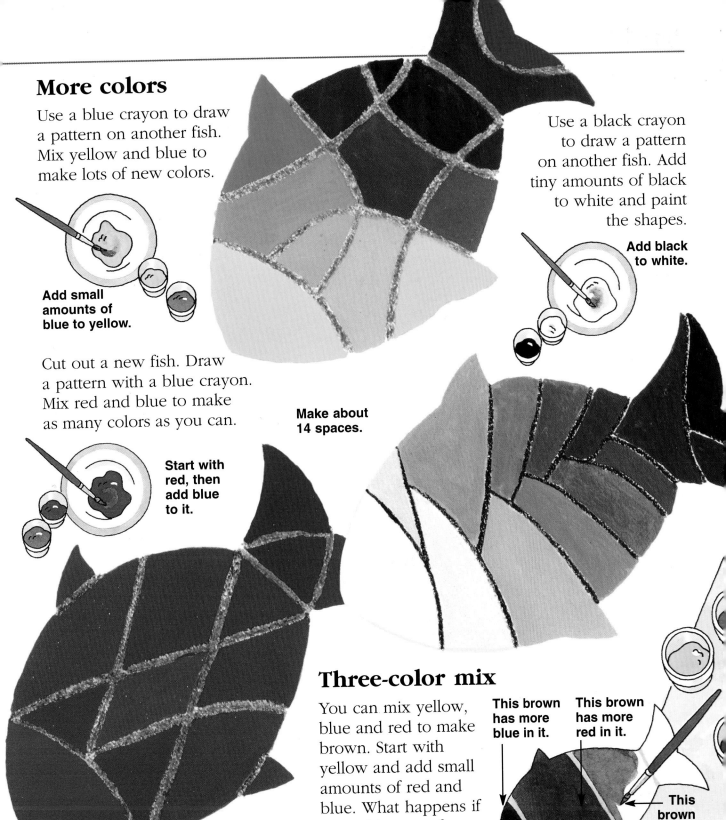

Add small amounts of blue to yellow.

Cut out a new fish. Draw a pattern with a blue crayon. Mix red and blue to make as many colors as you can.

Start with red, then add blue to it.

Make about 14 spaces.

Use a black crayon to draw a pattern on another fish. Add tiny amounts of black to white and paint the shapes.

Add black to white.

Three-color mix

You can mix yellow, blue and red to make brown. Start with yellow and add small amounts of red and blue. What happens if you add more of one color than another?

This brown has more blue in it.

This brown has more red in it.

This brown has more yellow in it.

Color blends

Painting colors so they mix into each other is called blending. The picture below has a blended background.

On these pages you need:
Letter size white paper
Paints
Thick and thin soft brushes
A big potato
A scrap of cardboard
Scissors
A rag or paper towel

Dark to light

Thick brush

Paint all the way across.

Prepare blue and white in pots. If you use powder paint, add water to it. Put some of the blue on a plate.

Lay the paper with its short edges at the sides. Paint a blue band across the top. Clean the brush in water.

Work quickly before the paint dries.

Brush the joint to make it disappear.

The lightness or darkness of a color is called its tone.

Primary blends

Yellow and red blend

Red and blue blend

Yellow and blue blend

Blend primary colors by following the steps on the left. Use two colors instead of blue and white.

Mix some white into the blue on the plate, to make it lighter. Paint a band slightly overlapping the first one.

Mix more white into the blue and paint another band. Make each band lighter than the last one, until you finish.

Sailing boats

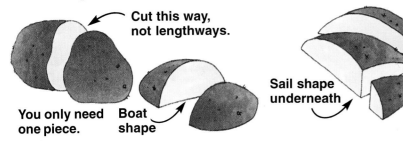

Cut this way, not lengthways.

You only need one piece.

Boat shape

Sail shape underneath

Cut a potato in half. Put one half with its cut side facing down. Cut it in half again. Ask an adult to help.

Take the piece left over from the boat shape. Cut a piece off the bottom. Cut off the curved side.

Paint a blue blend with a thick brush. Then turn the paper the other way around and leave it to dry.

Overlap some boats.

Wipe the shape before using a new color.

Thin brush

Mix a color for the boats. Paint the boat shape and press it onto the paper. Do lots of boats like this.

Print a colored sail on each boat. Start on the boats at the top, then work your way down the paper.

Fold a strip of cardboard lengthways. Dip the end in white paint and print waves. Paint lines on the boats.

Color-blend painting

You can do lots of different color blends in a painting. Blend pairs of colors, or blend a color and white.

On these pages you need:
Ledger size white paper
Ledger size piece of cardboard
Medium-thickness soft brush
Things to draw around
Scissors and glue stick
Self-adhesive plastic
Pencil and ruler
Paint

Make shapes overlap or touch.

If you use powder paint, mix water in on the plate.

Draw around things to make shapes on the paper. Draw your own shapes too. Do about six shapes altogether.

Prepare yellow, red, blue and white paint. Choose two colors to blend. Put a little of one on a plate.

Blend each new color into the last one.

Paint one end of a shape. Add the second color to the first, little by little. Fill more of the shape each time.

Remember to wash the brush in clean water.

Paint another shape with a different color blend. You could paint in a different direction this time.

Fill each shape with a blend. Work carefully, until the whole picture is full of blended color.

Multi-color jigsaw

Do a color-blend painting, or go to a photocopying business and get a color copy of your first painting.

Smooth out any bumps.

Put glue all over the back of the painting. Try not to miss any place. Stick it onto the cardboard. Leave it to dry.

Measure from the same edge each time.

Leftover piece

9.5cm (3¾in)

On the back, mark dots every 9.5cm (3¾in) on the long edges. Join the dots with a pencil and ruler.

Can you spot where the shapes and color blends match up?

See if your friends can do your jigsaw.

Bookmarks

Do a smaller painting. Glue it to cardboard and cut it into strips. Cover each one with self-adhesive plastic.

9.5cm (3¾in) — **Leftover piece**

Mark dots every 9.5cm (3¾in) along the short edges and join the dots. Then cut the squares out carefully.

Smooth out bubbles.

Make the plastic square bigger than the painted one.

Cut a square of self-adhesive plastic. Peel off the backing. Lay the plastic on the front of a jigsaw piece.

Snip the corners off the plastic. Fold the edges over and smooth out any bumps. Cover all the squares.

Thick paint

You can use paint thickly, so that it looks and feels bumpy, or "textured" when it dries. Paint used like this is called "impasto".

On these pages you need:
Paints and white glue*
A sketchbook or letter size paper
Ledger size sheet of paper
Thin, soft brush and a stiff brush
Flour, rice and a teaspoon
Pencil, ruler, round-ended knife
Scissors and a glue stick
Colored cardboard

Experiments

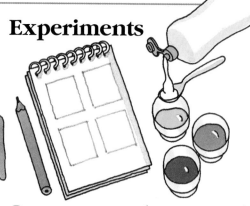

Draw squares on the paper or sketchbook. Put the paint in pots. Mix a teaspoonful of glue into each one.

Choose a color. Use the knife and plenty of paint to fill a square with thick, bumpy marks.

Thick paint frieze

Unfold and cut

Glue under here.

Fold the ledger size paper in half lengthways. Unfold it and cut along the crease. Glue two short edges together.

Mix a pale, runny color. Use a thin brush to paint a simple scene. Just paint the outlines of the shapes.

Mix plenty of paint on a plate before you add anything to it.

Clean tools before the paint dries on.

Decide which part to fill in first. Mix a color you like. Choose one of the ways of painting you tried above.

Textured cards

Make more textured squares and let them dry. Fold a rectangle of cardboard in half. Cut out the squares and glue some on the card in a pattern.

Paint color onto another square with a stiff brush. Scrape into it with the wooden end of the brush.

Mix a little rice into one color and flour into another. Paint these onto squares with a knife.

You could make lots of cards in different sizes.

Scrape into the paint before it dries.

You could try painting a second color onto parts that are wet.

Use colors that look good together.

Now paint another part in a different way. If you scrape into wet paint, paint and scrape a little at a time.

Paint each part of the picture in a new way. When it is dry, feel the bumpy patterns.

Color-match spirals

Mixing colors to match ones you can see is an important skill. You can practice it when you make the spirals on these pages.

On these pages you need:

Scraps of colored paper
from magazines
A sketchbook or letter size paper
Pencil, scissors and a glue stick
Big sheet of thin white cardboard
Strips of white paper
Paints and soft brushes
Needle and thread

Make piles of colors.

Tear colors from the scrap paper. Glue colors that look nice together in your sketchbook, in a trail.

If you use powder paint see page 6 for mixing reminders.

See pages 6 and 7 for reminders about making colors.

Medium-thickness brush

Draw a big spiral on the cardboard. Start in the middle and draw around and around four or five times.

Draw lines in different places on the spiral, to make lots of sections. Prepare your paints, too.

Which colors do you need for making the first one in your paper trail? Mix small amounts on a plate.

14

When you think you have made the color, paint a blob on a paper strip. Does it match the scrap?

Keep changing and testing the color to get the best match you can. Then paint the middle of the spiral.

Wash the plate if you run out of space.

Now try mixing the next color in the paper trail. Then paint the next section in your spiral.

Mix the colors in the paper trail one at a time. Each time you match a color, paint it in the spiral.

Thin brush

Thick brush

Color for back

When the spiral is dry, paint a pattern on each shape. Mix a new color for each pattern.

Paint the back one color and let it dry. Turn it over and cut out the spiral along the curling line.

Pattern facing down

Knot some thread and sew through the middle. Hang the spiral with the pattern facing down or up.

Hang your spiral from the ceiling or a door frame.

Pattern facing up

Make more spirals. Hang them on one thread.

You could decorate both sides of your spirals.

Look, paint and print

To paint something you can see, look very carefully. Make the shapes and colors as accurate as you can.

On these pages you need:
An orange cut in half around the middle, on a saucer
A sketchbook or white paper
A strip of white paper
Paints, brushes and scissors
A glue stick and adhesive
String and thick cardboard
Big sheets of white and colored paper

1

Thin brush

Make the shape life-size.

Mix a runny, light color on the plate. Look at the cut surface of the orange. Paint the shape of the outline.

2

Spaces between shapes

Skin

Segment shape

Paint lines to show the shapes you can see inside the orange. Can you see the things shown above?

3

Try different yellows or reds if you have them.

White for making light colors

Prepare the paints you need to make the colors in the orange. Then try mixing the lightest color you can see.

4

Look carefully to check which are the light parts.

Test the color on a paper strip. When it matches the orange's light parts, paint those parts on your picture.

5

Mix and test the color you need for the segments, then paint them. Do you need another color for the skin?

16

Fruity wrapping paper

Double line of string

Draw the shape of the orange on cardboard and cut it out. Glue a double line of string around the edge.

Cut out another shape the same size. Draw segments on it and cut them out. Glue them onto the first shape.

Cut a strip of cardboard. Fold it in half, then fold the ends outward. Tape it to the back of the shape.

Don't paint until the glue is dry.

Plenty of paint

Press all over the shape.

Paint the shape again for each new print.

Mix a color to match the segments in your painting. Paint it onto the printing block with a thick brush.

Press the block firmly onto a big sheet of paper, then take it off. Cover the whole sheet like this.

Print an orange and cut it out to make a gift tag.

Print a small piece of paper if you are wrapping a small present.

Overlap shapes. You could use a second color.

Try printing onto different colors.

Still life

A painting or drawing of a collection of things is called a still life. Here you can find out how to try to paint a still life yourself.

On these pages you need:
Letter size paper or bigger (colored or white)
A strip of paper the same color as the paper you paint on (for testing colors)
Thick and thin brushes
Paints
A collection of objects

Painting

1

Decide which way up to have the paper. Which way suits the arrangement best? Then mix a pale color.

Setting up

First, choose some things you would like to paint. Then find a place where you can arrange them and leave them. Start to place things together. Move them, add things or take them away until they look nice.

Try to have different colors in your arrangement.

You could use some patterned paper or cloth for extra interest.

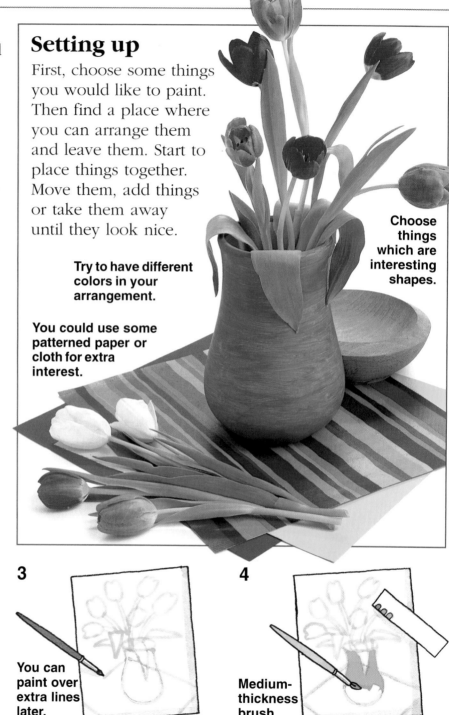

Choose things which are interesting shapes.

2

Use a thin brush to paint the shapes you see. Start with the outlines of the big, main shapes.

3

You can paint over extra lines later.

Then paint the shapes of smaller things. It may help to paint in lines where things overlap.

4

Medium-thickness brush

Decide what to paint first. Mix the main color and test it on the paper strip, next to the real thing.

5

You can paint over lines that you don't need.

When the paint dries, fill in more shapes. Test each color you mix before you use it. Add a background.

6

Can you see any shadows? Mix darker tones to paint these parts. Mix lighter tones for light parts.

7

Petal shapes

Veins on the leaves

When the paint is dry, look for shapes and details on the thing you are painting. Paint these in too.

8

If any of the things have patterns on them, add these last. A thin brush is best for delicate patterns.

Extra tips

Look at the things you are painting again and again while you work.

Mistakes don't matter. Just paint over them when the paint dries.

Leave your painting and come back to it, to see if you need to do more.

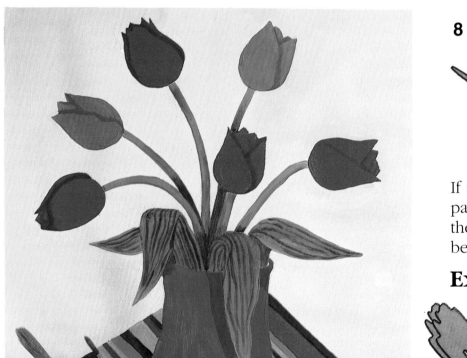

Painting people

A picture of a person is called a portrait. Ask someone to be your model, so you can paint their portrait. Make it as much like them as you can. Or look in a mirror and paint yourself instead. This is called a self-portrait.

On these pages you need:
Ledger size paper (colored or white)
A strip of paper the same color that you paint on
Letter size paper
Different thickness brushes
Paints
A mirror you can hold
A glue stick and colorful scraps of paper

Mini paintings

Make small paintings of your own eyes, nose and mouth by looking in the mirror, to get used to the shapes.

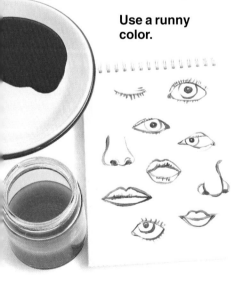

Use a runny color.

The portrait

1

Have the paper this way up.

Mix a pale, runny color. Paint the shape of your model's head, hair and shoulders. Use a thin brush.

2

Eyes are level with ears.

How wide is the mouth?

Look carefully at the eyes, ears, nose and mouth. Paint the shapes in. If your model has glasses, add these too.

3

Mix a color to match the skin. This can be tricky, so keep testing it. Paint the skin with a medium brush.

4

Can you see shadows around the nose, mouth and chin? If so, mix a darker tone and paint in these parts.

5

Mix a color to match the hair. Paint it to show which way it grows. Is it straight or curly? Does it stick out?

6

Mix the colors you need to paint the eyes. Paint them in with a thin brush. Paint the mouth and eyebrows too.

7

Paint your model's clothes. Can you copy the colors or patterns? Paint details like jewelry or glasses too.

8

Paint a colored background with a thick brush, or do a pattern. Paint around the portrait very carefully.

More ideas

Make a little self-portrait with a thin brush. Get some copies made at a copy store. Cut them out and glue them at the top of notepaper when you write to friends.

Glue colored scraps of paper onto a portrait to make colorful clothes.

Sponge and spatter

You can make colorful patterns by sponging or spattering paint onto paper.

On these pages you need:

Ledger size white paper
Paints and a pencil
Paintbrush for mixing
A small sponge
An old toothbrush
Scissors and a ruler
Mounting putty
A big piece of scrap cardboard
Newspaper and adhesive tape

Starry paper

1

Draw a star on cardboard. Cut it out. Draw around it lots of times to cover all the cardboard with stars.

2

Cut out the stars. Put a blob of mounting putty on each one. Press half of them gently onto the white paper.

3

Hold the star as you dab.

Blotchy marks look good.

Choose two colors. Mix plenty of the lightest one on a plate. Dip the sponge in. Dab around the stars.

4 Clean the plate first.

When the paint is dry, place the other stars in the spaces. Mix and sponge on the other color.

5

When the paint is dry, peel the stars off very carefully. See the bright pattern appear piece by piece.

Spattering

Spread lots of newspaper first.

Spattered paint looks more delicate than sponged paint.

Dip the toothbrush in the paint. Hold it over the paper and pull your finger along the bristles. Do this again and again.

More ideas

Position all the shapes at once. Sponge on the first color. Sponge another color lightly over the top.

Tear long strips of paper or newspaper. Lay them across the paper and tape them down. Sponge on color.

You could paint extra detail on top of shapes with a thin brush.

Think of different shapes you could use.

Stripes could go from top to bottom, from side to side or both.

Book covers

Open the book. Lay it on the bottom edge of some big patterned paper. Draw a line where the top comes to.

Cut off the extra piece at the top. Then fold the side pieces over the cover and press firmly along the folds.

Painting outdoors

To paint outdoors, take everything you need with you. The best way to do this is to make a painting kit. Take it on vacation, to a friend's house or into the park or backyard.

On these pages you need:

A small sketchbook or eight sheets of letter size paper (white and colored)
Pencil, ruler, thick needle, thread and scissors
Strong shoe box, long cardboard tube, elastic bands
Paints and five little plastic pots with lids
Brushes and a rag (or kitchen paper towel)
Two circles of material (about 12cm (3¾in) across)
Screw-top jar that fits in the box when the lid is on
Small plastic plate or lid of a plastic container

Homemade sketchbook

Short edges

7cm (2¾in)

14cm (5½in)

Fold eight sheets of paper in half, or cut bigger paper to letter size then fold it.

On each piece, mark dots 7cm (2¾in) and 14cm (5½in) along the fold.

Take a pencil for making notes.

Take a small sketchbook or make one yourself. Find out how above.

Paintbrushes go in this tube. Secure a circle of material over each end with an elastic band.

You may need to cut the end off the tube, so it fits in the box.

Take a rag or paper towel to dry brushes on.

Half fill each pot with paint. Put the lids on firmly.

Use a small plastic plate or the lid of a plastic container for mixing colors on.

Half fill the jar with water. Screw the lid on tightly.

Long thread

Leave the end sticking out.

Snip the ends off.

Use the thick needle to make holes where the dots are. Or ask an adult to help you.

Thread the needle. Poke it through the first hole while you hold all the paper.

Turn the paper over. Poke the needle down through the other hole.

Sew through the holes four times. Unthread the needle. Tie a double knot.

Things to paint

Here are some ideas for things you could paint. Can you think of some more?

You could paint over two whole pages.

Make a picture diary of things you see and do each day on vacation. You could write notes, too.

Paint flowers and insects in the yard.

Tips for using your kit

Use a ribbon or a big elastic band to hold the lid on the box.

Find a flat place to work and stand the pots in the lid.

Clean everything in your kit afterward, ready for next time.

Paint and stick

Making a picture by sticking on pieces of paper is called collage. Use collage and paint together, to make an imaginary jungle picture.

On these pages you need:
A big sheet of colored paper (ledger or bigger), or white paper painted with a blue or gray blended background
Paints, brushes, scissors, glue
An extra sheet of paper
Scraps of colored paper
Bowls (about seven)

1

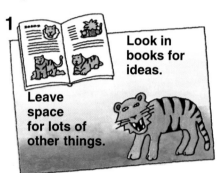

Look in books for ideas.

Leave space for lots of other things.

Paint an animal on the big paper. It could be a tiger or another wild animal, or you could make up your own.

2

You need big and small pieces.

Tear lots of different colors from your collection of scrap paper. Put a color group in each bowl.

3

Torn edges can look good.

How big is your plant going to be?

Decide where to put the first plant. Tear or cut out big leaves from the scrap collection. Glue them on.

4

Do another plant. Make the leaves a different shape this time. You could use a different color, too.

5

Use dark colors for shadows.

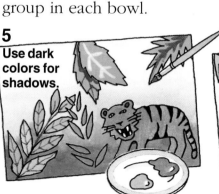

Add more plants. Some could hang down. Then paint in the stems and paint veins on the leaves.

6

Paint long grass to hide part of your animal, or stick on paper grass. The animal could be peeping out.

7

Add some bright jungle flowers. Paint them, or make them from colored paper. Do different kinds.

8

Paint colorful butterflies, birds, caterpillars, snakes and other creatures on a new piece of paper.

9

Cut the creatures out and stick them in the jungle. Add as much as you like. You could add more another day.

Use paint and paper to decorate a collection of jungle pots. Each pot could be different.

Jungle pots

Buy a terracotta flower pot from a garden center. Paint it to look like an animal's coat. You could do tiger stripes or leopard spots. Stick on leaves and flowers, then paint more details on top. You could ask an adult to varnish it for you.

Computer paintings

Different art programs let you make pictures on the computer screen. The programs do the same kinds of things. These pages tell you how to make pictures with the Microsoft® Paintbrush™ program which you use with Microsoft® Windows® software.

The display

A display on the computer screen shows you all the things you can use to make a picture.

These are different painting tools. You can choose which one to use.

Change the thickness of the mark you make by choosing one of these lines.

This shows the colors you can use. It is called the Palette.

First marks

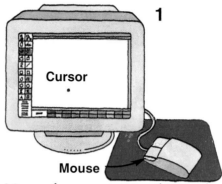

1

Cursor

Mouse

Move the mouse on the pad to move the dot on the screen called the cursor.

2

Tools

Click this button.

Move the cursor to the brush in the tools section. Click the left mouse button.

3

Part of the Palette.

Move the cursor to a color. Pick it by clicking the left mouse button.

4

To draw a new line, let go of the button and start in a new place.

Hold the button down.

Move the cursor to the middle. Move the mouse as you press its left button.

Draw and fill

Brush tool

Pick the Brush tool, then pick a color. Move the mouse to draw wiggly shapes on the screen.

Paint Roller tool

Fill each shape with a new color.

Pick the Paint Roller tool and a color. To fill a shape, move the cursor to it and click the left mouse button.

Brush thickness

Line thicknesses

Paint a picture using lots of different colors and line thicknesses.

Painting ideas

Experiment with more tools. Then make paintings using the skills you have learned. Here are a few ideas.

Stormy sea

Spray paint

Airbrush tool

Pick the Airbrush tool. Use it to spray different colors and patterns.

Ask someone to show you how to save your paintings.

Party time

Amazing plants and flowers

You don't have to make the paintings very realistic.

More ideas

If you have a color printer, print out your favorite paintings.

There are shops which do color photocopies onto T-shirts. You could get one of your paintings copied. This is fairly expensive, but it makes a good present.

Artists and paintings

Everyone has their own way of doing things. Here are some of the different things artists do when they paint.

They stand back to look at their painting. This helps them decide what to do to it next.

They sometimes have a rest and do something else instead. Then they do more to the painting.

They paint over parts of the picture and make changes, until they are happy with it.

Some artists take an hour to do a painting. Other artists take weeks, months or even years.

Artists often make more than one painting at a time. They do a little of one, then a little of another.

Some artists paint things on the spot. Others make lots of rough drawings and paintings first. They look at these later, to help them do a finished painting.

Finding paintings

You can see paintings in art galleries or museums. An art gallery is a room or a building where you can see works of art. Most towns have one.

You can find books of paintings in libraries, bookstores and art galleries. Real paintings are photographed, then the photographs are put in books.

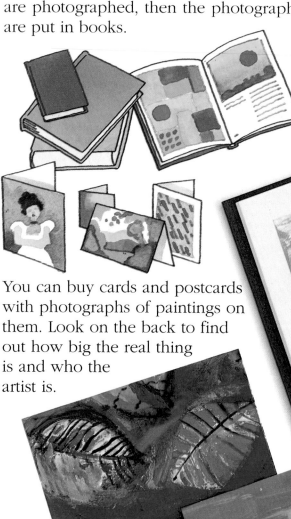

You can buy cards and postcards with photographs of paintings on them. Look on the back to find out how big the real thing is and who the artist is.

Looking at paintings

Here are some questions you can ask yourself when you see a painting you like.

What can I see in the picture?

How does the painting make me feel?

Has the artist made the paint look bumpy or smooth?

Can I see the brush marks?

Who made the painting and how big is it?

Artists and skills

Here are some artists who used painting skills you have learned in this book. The dates tell you when the artists lived. Can you find any of their paintings to look at?

Jackson Pollock (1912-1956) made his paintings by spattering and dribbling paint. Some of his paintings are enormous.

Wassily Kandinsky (1866-1944) made some paintings full of blended color. They had lots of shapes in them.

Vincent van Gogh (1853-1890) used thick, bright paint. His brush marks make swirling patterns. He often took his painting kit out and made paintings on the spot.

Vincent van Gogh also painted portraits. He painted many self-portraits too.

Paul Cézanne (1839-1906) painted lots of still lifes.

31

Index

Acknowledgements

Page 28: Microsoft and Windows are registered trademarks, and Paintbrush is a trademark of the Microsoft Corporation.

Usborne Publishing Ltd. would like to thank the following children for the use of their paintings in this book: Amy Jordan, Kate Squire and Lydia Squire.

Thanks also to Catherine Figg for the use of her work.

First published in 1996 by Usborne Publishing Ltd, Usborne House, 83-85 Saffron Hill, London EC1N 8RT, England. Copyright © 1996 Usborne Publishing Ltd.

The name Usborne and the device ♛ are Trade Marks of Usborne Publishing Ltd. All rights reserved.

No part of this publication may be reproduced, stored in a retrieval system or transmitted in any form or by any means, electronic, mechanical, photocopying, recording or otherwise, without prior permission of the publisher. AE. First published in America in August 1996. Printed in Belgium.

More artists

Here is a list of some famous artists. Can you find any of their paintings to look at?

Salvador Dalí
Robert Delaunay
Paul Gauguin
Patrick Heron
Fernand Léger
Roy Lichtenstein
Henri Matisse
Claude Monet
Pablo Picasso
Bridget Riley
Henri Rousseau
Georges Seurat